The Sporty Fairies

For Gemma Poole,
with lots of love

Special thanks to
Sue Mongredien

ORCHARD BOOKS
338 Euston Road, London NW1 3BH
Orchard Books Australia
Level 17/207 Kent Street, Sydney, NSW 2000
A Paperback Original

First published in 2008 by Orchard Books.

© 2008 Rainbow Magic Limited.
A HIT Entertainment company. Rainbow Magic
is a trademark of Rainbow Magic Limited.
Reg. U.S. Pat. & Tm. Off. And other countries.

HiT entertainment

Illustrations © Orchard Books 2008

A CIP catalogue record for this book is available
from the British Library.

ISBN 978 1 84616 894 9
1 3 5 7 9 10 8 6 4 2

Printed and bound in China by Imago

Orchard Books is a division of Hachette Children's Books,
an Hachette UK company

www.hachette.co.uk

Gemma
the Gymnastics
Fairy

by Daisy Meadows

ORCHARD BOOKS

www.rainbowmagic.co.uk

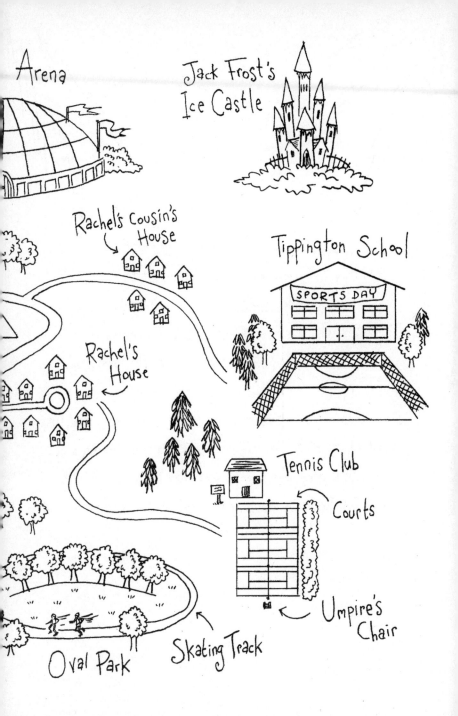

The Fairyland Olympics are about to start,
And my crafty goblins are going to take part.
We'll win this year, for I've got a cunning plan.
I'm sending my goblins to the arena in Fairyland.

The Magic Sporty Objects that make sports safe and fun,
Will be stolen by my goblins, to keep until we've won.
Sporty Fairies, prepare to lose and to watch us win.
Goblins, follow my commands, and let the games begin!

Contents

Someone in School

"Almost there," Rachel Walker said as she and her best friend, Kirsty Tate, walked along the sunny street. "Aunty Joan lives around the corner, near my school."

"That's good," Kirsty said, glancing down at the basket they were carrying. "These Easter eggs might melt if it was any further!"

Kirsty was staying with Rachel's family for a week of the Easter holidays and the two girls were delivering Easter gifts to Rachel's cousins.

"I can't believe it's Friday already," Rachel said. "The Fairyland Olympic Games start today!"

Kirsty nodded. "And we still haven't found Gemma the Gymnastics Fairy's Magic Hoop," she said. "If we don't get it back from the goblins soon, then all the gymnastics events at the Olympics will be spoiled."

The girls were having a very exciting week, helping the Sporty Fairies find their missing Magic Sporty Objects. The Magic Sporty Objects ensured that sport was fun and safe for everyone in the human world, as well as in Fairyland, but only if they were with their rightful owners, the Sporty Fairies.

Naughty Jack Frost knew the Magic Sporty Objects were so powerful that they made anyone who was holding them, or even just close to them, very skilled at that particular sport. He had sent his goblins to steal the Sporty Objects so that they could use them to cheat in the Olympic Games and become the winning team. Jack Frost knew that the winners would receive a golden cup full of luck as the big prize – and he really wanted it for himself.

The goblins had brought the Magic Sporty Objects into the human world to use while they practised their sports. As the Magic Sporty Objects weren't where they were supposed to be, sports in Fairyland and the human world had been disrupted and spoiled.

The girls passed Tippington School, and Kirsty suddenly stopped. "That's strange," she said, staring across the playground. "I've just seen some children inside the school, dressed in green."

"School's closed for the holidays," Rachel told her. "And our uniform is blue and grey."

The same thought struck both girls at the same time, and they let out a gasp. "Goblins!" cried Rachel.

"If they are goblins, they might have Gemma's Magic Hoop with them," Kirsty said excitedly.

They gazed at the school, but there was no sign of anyone in there now. "Let's drop these Easter eggs off quickly, then look around properly," Rachel suggested.

She and Kirsty rushed to Rachel's aunt's house. They knocked on the door, but there was no reply, so they set the basket down in the porch, out of the sun.

Then they hurried back to the school.
The main entrance was locked. "Let's
try round the back," Rachel said,
leading the way. Then she and Kirsty
froze as they heard the sound of
someone whistling.

They peered around the wall to see
a man with his back to them, painting
some bookcases. "It's the caretaker,"
Rachel whispered. "Look, he's left the
door open. Let's sneak in."

Hearts pounding, the girls crept in through the open door.

"It's very quiet," Kirsty commented. "Maybe I imagined it."

"Well, let's check out the gym while we're here," Rachel said. "Follow me."

Rachel led Kirsty down a long corridor until they reached a door. "This is where the gym equipment is stored," she said. "We can go through here into the gym itself."

She opened the door and a netball rolled out.

Frowning, Rachel picked it up and went inside. "What a mess!" she said in surprise. "It's never usually like this."

Kirsty followed. A pile of gym mats had been knocked over, there were balls scattered everywhere and some goal posts lay on the floor. Her heart thumped with excitement. People inside the school, mess in the gym cupboard… Something strange was definitely going on!

The girls crossed to the other door, opened it a crack and peeped out. Kirsty stifled a gasp. She couldn't believe her eyes. The gymnasium was a blur of green. There were goblins everywhere!

Training Time

The two girls stared in silence.
There were goblins swinging from
the parallel bars, and from rings
that dangled from the ceiling.
Other goblins were leaping over
the vault, dancing along the
balance beam and tumbling
across the floor mats.

"Wow," Kirsty said, unable to drag her eyes away. "They're brilliant! The Magic Hoop must be nearby for all the goblins to be performing so well!"

Rachel nodded. Then her eye was caught by a flash of blue, and she nudged Kirsty. "Look!" she hissed, pointing.

Kirsty turned, and saw a goblin effortlessly twirling a bright blue hoop around one arm. The hoop shimmered with blue sparkles. "That definitely looks like fairy magic," she breathed excitedly.

The goblin set the hoop rolling across one of the gym mats, while he performed a series of flawless back flips alongside it. Then he landed on 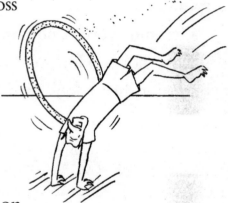 his feet, grabbed the hoop and bowed deeply to an imaginary audience.

"That must be Gemma's hoop," Rachel whispered. "The last Magic Sporty Object!"

"There's something sparkling in here, too," Kirsty said, suddenly noticing a tiny flash of light in a dark corner.

Rachel turned to see Gemma the Gymnastics Fairy come spiralling up out of a pile of hoops, in a burst of yellow sparkles.

Gemma wore a pale blue leotard and yellow tights. Her hair was coiled up in a bun, and her wings were tipped with gold.

"Hello, Gemma!" Kirsty said in delight. "Perfect timing – we think we've spotted your hoop."

Gemma beamed. "Hurrah!" she said. "I've just come from Fairyland, where all the athletes are busy with their last-minute practice sessions. The opening celebrations for the Olympics will be starting soon. We just have to get my hoop back in time!"

"Yes, the goblins are practising too," Kirsty remarked.

But Rachel was lost in thought. Gemma's and Kirsty's words had given her an idea. "That's it!" she cried. "We could help the goblins practise!"

Kirsty stared at her, wondering if she'd heard correctly. "Help the goblins?" she repeated in surprise.

Rachel grinned. "If we offer to train the goblins, we'll have a good chance of getting close to Gemma's hoop," she explained.

Gemma cartwheeled through the air.

"Yes!" she cried. "And we might even teach them that you can get better at a sport without having to cheat. You just need to practise!" She smiled. "Now, let's see…I know how I can help." She waved her wand at the girls, and golden fairy dust streamed around them. Then, in the twinkling of an eye, their clothes changed.

Rachel and Kirsty looked at each other and smiled. They were now wearing matching tracksuits and trainers, with stopwatches on their wrists. Their hair had been swept up into ponytails, and there were silver whistles around their

necks. Peaked caps helped to hide the girls' faces, so that the goblins wouldn't easily see through their disguise. "Look at our T-shirts!" Kirsty giggled, pointing. Rachel looked  down and saw that "K & R Goblin Training Team" was written in glittery silver letters across her chest.

Gemma flew up to perch on Kirsty's ponytail, where her wings made her look rather like a shiny hair bow. "Now to start training those goblins," she said. "And get the Magic Hoop!"

"Let's go," Kirsty agreed. And she and Rachel pushed open the doors and strode into the gym, blowing their whistles loudly.

The goblins all stopped in surprise. One goblin was so startled, he lost concentration during his floor routine and tumbled head over heels onto the crash mat. He picked himself up and shuffled over to another goblin. "Who are they?" the girls heard him whisper.

"All right, goblins!" shouted Kirsty. "This is your last chance to get in shape before the Fairyland Olympics! And we're going to help you, so line up in front of me! Move it! Move it!"

Rachel held her breath. For their plan to work, the goblins had to want her and Kirsty to help with their training. But none of the goblins had moved a muscle to line up. Was the plan doomed before it had even started?

Gymnastic Fantastic

"Come on!" Rachel cried, clapping her hands. "You don't want those fairies to beat you in the Olympics, do you? We're here to make you gymnastic fantastic, so that you have a chance of winning gold medals!"

"I want a medal!" one goblin called out from the crowd, running to start a line in front of Kirsty.

"Me too!" cried another.

"And me, and me!" called some
of the other goblins, as they jostled
to get in line.

The one with the Magic Hoop was
in the middle and demanded that the
others give him more room. "Look at
me!" he cried, swivelling the hoop
around his hips at lightning speed.

"We want you all to practise your back flips first," Rachel said. "You can demonstrate," she added, pointing at the goblin with the Magic Hoop.

She held her breath as the goblin walked to the edge of the mat. She'd noticed the way he'd let go of the hoop when he'd practised his back flips earlier. If he did the same thing again, she might be able to grab it!

As Rachel had hoped, the goblin set
the Magic Hoop rolling before flipping
along next to it.
Unfortunately,
the hoop whizzed
along so fast, it
was impossible
for Rachel and
Kirsty to even
think about
running to catch it.

And as soon as the goblin had finished,
he snatched it up again.

Kirsty and Rachel exchanged glances.
They'd have to try again later.

"OK, who's next?" Rachel asked.

"Me! Me! ME!" shouted the goblins,
trying to push each other out of
the way.

Kirsty blew her whistle. "It's you next," she decided, pointing to a goblin with a pointy chin. "Off you go!"

One by one, the goblins took turns to perform their back flips across the floor. They weren't quite as good as the goblin with the Magic Hoop, but they all tried hard.

Meanwhile, the goblin with the Magic Hoop was showing off to a group of goblins in a corner of the gym. "Watch this!" he yelled, breaking into a run across the gym floor. He ran to the gym horse and vaulted over it, tossing the hoop high into the air as he did so. He turned a perfect somersault and then landed

feet-first through the falling hoop.

Everyone burst into applause, including Kirsty, Rachel and Gemma.

"He won't be able to do that in the Olympic contest," Rachel heard one goblin mutter to another. "Jack Frost is going to shrink the hoop really small so the judges don't know he's got it. Clever, huh?"

Gemma bristled
with annoyance.
"I can't bear
cheating," she
whispered to
Kirsty. "It makes
me feel sick!"

But watching the
performance had given
Kirsty an idea. "Let's make an obstacle
course for the goblins," she suggested.
"You saw how the goblin had to throw
the Magic Hoop when he vaulted.
Well, there are other gym moves where
he'd have to let it go, too."

Rachel's eyes lit up. "Yes," she said,
"and we could even end the course
with a ring toss – where the goblins
have to throw a hoop over me or you.

Then the goblin with the Magic Hoop
will have to throw it right to us!"

"Brilliant!" cried Gemma, in her
silvery voice. "Let's put the plan
into action!"

Overcoming Obstacles

Kirsty blew her whistle again. "You did a great job on your back flips," she told the goblins. "Now we're going to set up an obstacle course for you. Please practise your forward and backward rolls while we do that."

The goblins immediately began rolling around on the floor, pausing every so often to argue with each other.

Meanwhile, Kirsty and Rachel quickly arranged some pieces of equipment to make an obstacle course, then Rachel clapped her hands to get the goblins' attention. "This is what you need to do," she said.

"Start by walking on your hands along the balance beam. Then run over to the parallel bars and do three somersaults."

"Next," Kirsty said, "you turn upside down on the rings, vault over the horse and tumble across the mat while twirling a ribbon."

"Finally," Rachel explained, "each of you has to toss a hoop over Kirsty,

who'll be standing at the other
end of the gym." She held up her
stopwatch. "I'll time you all.
I wonder who'll be the fastest?"

"I'll be the fastest," a tall goblin
boasted. "You wait!"

"No way!" a goblin with big ears
argued. "I'll be faster than you."

Kirsty pointed to a small goblin at
the front. "You can go first," she said
encouragingly. "Ready,
steady, go!"

Rachel started her
stopwatch as the
small goblin set off.
He flipped into a
handstand and
carefully walked
along the balance beam.

His legs wobbled slightly but he
managed not to fall. Then he ran to
the parallel bars and performed three
somersaults – but he was
enjoying himself so
much that he
kept on going.
"Wheeee!" he
squealed, whizzing round.

"OK, onto the rings now," Rachel
reminded him.

The goblin swung upside-down on
the rings, then vaulted over the horse.
Then he grabbed a ribbon and began
a series of cartwheels and handsprings
across the mat, spiralling the ribbon as
he went. Unfortunately, he lost his
balance several times, and dropped his
ribbon once on the last section.

"Not to worry," Rachel said. "We can work on that later. Now grab a hoop from the pile, stand behind the line and take your best shot."

The goblin took a hoop, steadied himself and then threw it towards Kirsty. The hoop bounced off Kirsty's arm and clattered to the floor.

"Good try," Kirsty called.

"Your time was three minutes, thirty seconds," Rachel told him. "Next!"

It took a while for all the goblins to go through the course. The goblin with the Magic Hoop insisted on going last. "What's the fastest time so far?" he asked as he stood at the starting line.

"Two minutes, forty seconds," Rachel replied.

The goblin looked scornful. "I'll beat that easily!" he declared.

"Ready, steady, go!" Rachel called, blowing her whistle.

Off went the goblin, mounting the beam with a spectacular leap. He tossed the hoop into the air as he went into

a handstand and caught it on one foot, balancing it perfectly as he moved along the beam. "Wow!" Kirsty muttered under her breath to Gemma. "That's impressive."

At the end of the beam, the goblin
dismounted with a double back flip,
sending the hoop
flying into the air.
As he landed, he
caught it neatly
and then ran on
to the parallel bars.

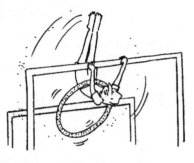

With the hoop looped
over one shoulder, he did three perfect
somersaults at dizzying speed.

It was quite a show. The goblin
whizzed through the rest of the
obstacle course without a single
mistake. The other goblins watched
open-mouthed, too amazed even
to argue with each other.

He was making record time when
he came to the last part of the

challenge – the ring toss. He looked
suspiciously at Kirsty and held tight to
the Magic Hoop. "Hoop-tossing is not
a gymnastic sport," he said. "I shan't
do this bit."

Kirsty bit her lip. She had to think
of something fast, otherwise their plan
would fail! She shrugged. "Oh, dear,"
she said pityingly. "Are you worried
you won't be as good as the others?"

"No way!" the goblin snapped. "Watch this!" And he tossed the hoop high into the air.

The girls and Gemma held their breath as it spun in mid-air above Kirsty's head...

Frost in Fairyland

The hoop landed perfectly over Kirsty's
head and the goblins all burst into a
round of applause.

The goblin who'd thrown it smirked
and bowed and then walked towards
Kirsty as if to take it back.

But Kirsty was too quick for him.
She stepped out of the hoop, picked it

up and held it in the air for Gemma, who zoomed down to it immediately. As soon as Gemma's fingers closed around it, the hoop magically shrank down to its Fairyland size. Then Gemma touched it with her wand, and there was a flash of golden sparkles. The hoop's magic was working properly again!

"Hey!" cried one of the goblins.
"It's one of those meddling fairies – and
she's got our hoop!"

"Someone get it back!" yelled another
goblin. "Otherwise we'll never win
anything at the Olympics!"

The goblins all made a mad dash for
the girls and Gemma, clambering over
each other in their
rush to get the
hoop. Kirsty
and Rachel
looked at
one another
in alarm
as the mob
of angry
goblins surged
towards them,

but Gemma waved her wand and
turned the girls into fairies,
just in time. Rachel's
heart thumped as she
fluttered out of the
goblins' reach.
That was close!

Gemma waved
her wand again,
and all the
pieces of gym
equipment
sparkled with
thousands of tiny
golden lights before
dancing back into
their rightful places in
the store room. The
goblins watched in

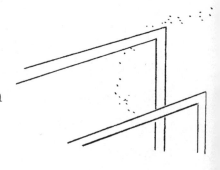

bewilderment, their eyes wide. As the last hoop rolled away, Gemma grinned at them. "See you in Fairyland," she said. "Don't be late – or you'll miss the opening ceremony of the Olympics!" Before any of the goblins could reply, Gemma had waved her wand a third time, and she and the girls were swept up in a magical whirlwind.

"Off we go to Fairyland!" Kirsty and Rachel heard her call merrily.

A few seconds later, the girls felt themselves float down to land, and the whirlwind cleared.

"We're in the Fairyland Arena again!" Kirsty declared.

Rachel whistled. "And look how full it is."

The girls had been in the arena
once already, on the first day of this
adventure. But then it had been
completely empty, whereas now the
seats were filled with excited-looking
fairies, elves, pixies and goblins, all
chattering about the Olympics.

Kirsty could quite happily have
spent ages gazing around at the sights.
A tall green frog was selling official
programmes on one row. A group
of pixie cheerleaders danced in the
centre of the arena. And the spectators
all waved colourful flags and banners
to show which contestants they
were supporting. Some of the flags
were magical and kept changing
colour. Some even seemed to be
playing tunes!

They'd landed at the side of the arena and Gemma led them to the centre, where the Fairy King and Queen greeted them warmly. Then the King handed Gemma a sparkly gold microphone, so that she could speak to the crowd.

"Hello, everyone," Gemma said, waving. "I'm pleased to announce that Kirsty and Rachel have now helped us get all the

Magic Sporty Objects back, including my Magic Hoop!"

A huge cheer went up from the spectators, but not from the watching goblins. They looked decidedly fed up at the news. But the fairies, pixies, elves and other magical people were all clapping, cheering and waving their flags with joy.

GOBLINZ TO WIN!

The King and Queen looked
delighted, too. "Thank you," King
Oberon said to Kirsty and Rachel.
"You have helped save our Olympic
Games! Without you, the goblins would
have had an unfair advantage."

"Now that the Magic Sporty Objects
are back with our Sporty Fairies, the
games will be fairly contested," Queen
Titania smiled.
"We are very grateful."

Kirsty and Rachel curtsied,
feeling very proud.
But then the air
turned cold. Rachel
shivered and rubbed
her arms. "Where's
that wind coming
from?" she asked,

as an icy gale blew through the arena.

"There's frost on the ground!" Kirsty exclaimed, pointing to the white sparkly crystals at their feet.

Everyone stared up at the sky as a figure approached, speeding through the air.

"It's Jack Frost!" Rachel realised in dismay.

Beginnings and Endings

Jack Frost landed in the arena and
stamped his feet. "If it hadn't been
for you interfering, I'd have won
the Olympics this year," he snarled
at Kirsty and Rachel. "The golden cup
of luck would have been mine!"

The Queen gave him a stern look.
"Your team will have to play by the

rules like every other team in the games," she told him.

Jack Frost ignored her and advanced on the girls, his wand raised. "I'm fed up with you two messing up my plans," he shouted. He pointed his wand at them. "So now I'm going to—"

"You're not going to do anything!" the Queen interrupted, waving her own wand. The crowd gasped as Jack Frost's wand flew straight into the Queen's hand.

"I'll look after this while the games are taking place," she told Jack Frost firmly. "I'm not going to let you disrupt the Olympics any further!"

Jack Frost scowled at her, but without his wand he could do nothing except turn and storm off to the spectators' area.

"He knows when he's beaten," Gemma said in a low voice.

"And now the games can begin!" the King declared.

Gemma winked at the girls. "That's my cue," she said, and shot up into the air. She was joined by the other six Sporty Fairies – Helena, Francesca, Zoe, Naomi, Samantha and Alice – and they all spiralled up towards the clouds.

Rachel and Kirsty watched as they then flew back to the arena in an amazing rainbow of colour. They sprinkled fairy dust over the athletes lining up for the opening parade, then wrote "GOOD LUCK!" in large glittery letters in the sky.

"Please be upstanding for the singing of the Fairyland Olympic Anthem," Queen Titania said, and the audience rose to their feet.

A goblin walked to the centre of the stage, with a microphone in his hand. He cleared his throat and began to sing.

Rachel elbowed Kirsty and grinned. "It's the goblin we met when we helped Rebecca the Rock 'n' Roll Fairy," she whispered. "Remember?"

Kirsty nodded. "Yes, the one who loved to sing Elvis songs!" she said with a grin.

The goblin made a sweeping bow as he finished singing, and the crowd cheered – Rachel and Kirsty loudest of all.

Then the Queen presented the girls with a glittering silver wand. "Girls, we would be honoured if you would light the Olympic flame for us," she said. "And there are some fairies who would love to help you…"

As she finished speaking, Rachel and Kirsty both gasped. Flying into the arena was Ruby the Red Fairy, the first fairy they'd ever met, with her Rainbow sisters. Behind them came all the Weather Fairies, and then Katie the Kitten Fairy flew in, waving at the girls as she was joined by the other Pet Keeper Fairies. More and more of

the girls' fairy friends kept flying into
the arena.

Kirsty couldn't stop smiling as she
greeted them all. "I think every fairy
we've ever helped is here with us,"
she said happily to Rachel.

Rachel had a lump in her throat.
"It's so nice to see you again!" she said,
throwing her arms around Lucy the
Diamond Fairy.

Once all the fairies had arrived, the Queen commanded them to touch their wands together, along with the silver wand that Rachel and Kirsty were holding.

Rachel held her breath as all the wands came together. A spark appeared at the end of the special silver wand.

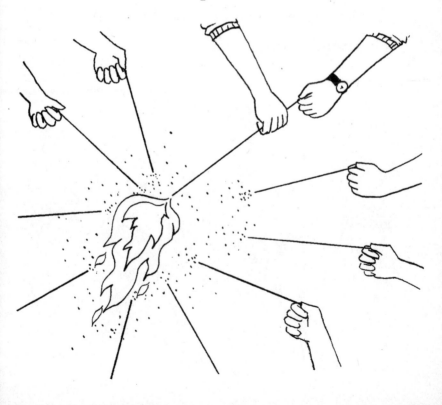

Then the other fairies moved aside
and the girls took the lit wand towards
a sparkling silver cauldron.
They touched the flame
to the cauldron,
and, in a flash of
rainbow-coloured
sparkles, a
roaring flame
flared up and
then settled
down to burn steadily.

There was a round of
applause from the crowd
and the fairies flew up into the air
again, calling out their goodbyes.

King Oberon and Queen Titania
came over to the girls. "It's time for
you to go home now," the King said,

"but you'll find one last surprise waiting for you there."

"Thank you," Kirsty said, curtseying.

"We've really enjoyed helping the Sporty Fairies," added Rachel. "We're all very grateful to you," the Queen said. "Goodbye, girls!"

"Goodbye!" Rachel and Kirsty replied.

Then the King waved his wand, and the girls were swept up in a whirlwind and carried gently home.

They found themselves outside Rachel's school, in their normal clothes, each holding a gold sparkly envelope.

Kirsty opened hers eagerly, as did Rachel. Inside they found glittering silver tickets. "'All-access pass to the Fairyland Olympics'," Kirsty read aloud.

"Wow!" Rachel said, beaming. "We can go to any event we like."

"Oh!" Kirsty marvelled. "What a great surprise!"

A light gust of wind made the tickets flutter in their fingers, and they heard Gemma's silvery voice carried on the breeze. "All you have to do is hold your ticket and wish, and you'll be back at the Fairyland Arena," she whispered.

Kirsty and Rachel smiled in delight. "I'm so pleased we'll get to see the events," Rachel said happily, as they started to walk home.

"Me too," Kirsty agreed. "I especially want to see how the goblin gymnastics team perform. After all, they did have some excellent coaching!"

Win Rainbow Magic Goodies!

There are lots of Rainbow Magic fairies, and we want to know
which one is your favourite! Send us a picture of her and tell
us in thirty words why she is your favourite and why you like
Rainbow Magic books. Each month we will put the entries into
a draw and select one winner to receive a Rainbow Magic
Sparkly T-shirt and Goody Bag!

Send your entry on a postcard to Rainbow Magic Competition,
Orchard Books, 338 Euston Road, London NW1 3BH.
Australian readers should email: childrens.books@hachette.com.au
New Zealand readers should write to Rainbow Magic Competition,
4 Whetu Place, Mairangi Bay, Auckland NZ.
Don't forget to include your name and address.
Only one entry per child.

Good luck!

The Music Fairies

The Sporty Fairies have got their
magic objects back. Now Rachel and
Kirsty must help the Music Fairies,
starting with

Poppy the Piano Fairy

A Musical Message

"Ooh, I love to dance!" Rachel Walker sang along to the radio, pretending her hairbrush was a microphone. "When I hear the music, my toes start tapping and my fingers start snapping - I just love to dance!"

Kirsty Tate, Rachel's best friend, grinned and grabbed her own hairbrush.

"I can't stop dancing!" she chorused. "Just can't stop dancing!"

The girls tried to do a complicated dance routine as they sang, but then Kirsty went left and Rachel went right and they ended up bumping into each other. Laughing, they collapsed onto Kirsty's bedroom carpet.

"It's really hard to sing and dance at the same time," said Rachel as the song ended.

"I know," Kirsty agreed. "I don't think we'd be very good in a band, Rachel!"

"That was The Sparkle Girls with their new single, *Can't Stop Dancing*," the radio DJ announced as Kirsty and Rachel sat up. "And if anyone out there thinks they could make it big as a pop star too, why not come along and audition for the National Talent Competition next weekend?"

Rachel and Kirsty glanced at each other.

"That sounds cool!" Rachel said.

"One lucky singer or band will win

a recording contract with MegaBig
Records," the DJ went on. "So remember
– come along to the New Harmony
Mall next weekend, and maybe one day
I'll be playing *your* songs on my show!"

"The New Harmony Mall is only a
few miles from Wetherbury," Kirsty said.
"I'm sure Mum or Dad would take us
to watch the competition if we asked
them..."

Read the rest of

Poppy the Piano Fairy

to find out what magic happens next...

Have you checked out the

website at:

www.rainbowmagic.co.uk

RAINBOW magic®
The Music Fairies

POPPY
THE PIANO FAIRY
978-1-40830-033-6

ELLIE
THE GUITAR FAIRY
978-1-40830-030-5

FIONA
THE FLUTE FAIRY
978-1-40830-029-9

DANNI
THE DRUM FAIRY
978-1-40830-028-2

MAYA
THE HARP FAIRY
978-1-40830-031-2

VICTORIA
THE VIOLIN FAIRY
978-1-40830-027-5

SADIE
THE SAXOPHONE FAIRY
978-1-40830-032-9

Out now!